WHAT I LOST IN HIS GRAVE

WHAT I LOST IN HIS GRAVE

RAGINI GUPTA

PARTRIDGE

Print information available on the last page.

To order additional copies of this book, contact
Partridge India
000 800 10062 62
orders.india@partridgepublishing.com

www.partridgepublishing.com/india

For Sumani, without whom this book wouldn't exist

William

I can feel the Agrenalin working its way through my bloodstream. Instantly, the heavy weight of cancer that has been crushing my body inside out starts to drift away.

My tense muscles begin to relax as I gulp in the soothing autumn breeze coming through my square window. I had almost forgotten what it feels like to breathe without an arrow piercing through my oesophagus.

I'm fading away. This is what floating around the moon must feel like.

As my eyelids gently slide down, a wave of guilt hits me. I begin to panic, trying my best to fight against the Agrenalin, but it's too late.

Am I really about to do this to Caitlyn?

At least my parents won't suspect suicide.

Caitlyn

Chapter I

The most effective way for me to soothe my attention deficit hyperactive nerves is by going for endless walks. For me, the best time to walk is during the brisk period of transformation from autumn to winter, which gives me a certain high by shooting my spirits up to the roof of the exosphere.

If the seasons were humans, they would all have their own drastically different characteristics; all except for autumn, which would just be your average Joe—the one who's neither here nor there. But if you look at autumn from the perspective of a season (especially when it's transforming into winter), it has an unattainable dazzling golden frosted beauty. Although in a world where seasons are humans autumn would be underrated and ordinary, I find comfort in thinking that in it's alternate world of seasons, autumn is nothing but extraordinary.

I love walking on an autumn-winter transformation day as small gulps of rustic air inundate my nasal cavity, while crisp golden brown leaves crackle and swirl around my legs.

Since the weather requires me to put on a coat, I find it easier to get lost in the world of my thoughts. When I wear a coat with my arms wrapped around the top of my waist, I feel protected. Without my coat, I feel as though my thoughts may be exposed to the rest of the world.

In terms of the weather, the day could not have gotten better. Most people dislike London weather because they find it erratic. I, on the other hand, love it for its erraticism. I believe that the unpredictable nature of the weather is what keeps the city bustling and alive.

I was with my handsome 75-pound Labrador, Cinder, whose fur was an in-between shade of brown and golden. The blaze in his warmth-filled eyes reminded me of a bonfire. We quietly walked toward our favourite hill (we even gave it the name 'Hill'), which looked upon a deserted fort. The top of Hill's conical frustum-shaped structure was like a semi-circular crater. Its depth not only hid us from everyone else, but also managed to provide us with a decent view of our subtly lit neighbourhood.

Cinder and I found Hill the day we started going out for walks when Cinder was just a tiny puff of golden fur. It was love at first sight. It was one of those days where I needed to get my feelings out on sheets of paper in the form of songs. I had my guitar, Felix (I name my instruments as well), my notebook, and my little puff of fur. When I saw Hill, I knew that his semi-circular crater was the place I'd like to nestle in every single day.

Today, just like every other day, I had Felix and my notebook with me. On reaching Hill, we went straight up to the spot where I kept a foldable chair along with a small electric lantern and solar-powered fairy lights.

I got Felix's case off of my shoulder and sat down cross-legged. For what seemed to be five minutes, but was probably half an hour, all I did was stare at the fort that stood on the opposite side with Cinder's head on my lap.

There was so much going on in my head; I was infuriated, frightened, and depressed all at once. This range of extreme emotions made me oblivious toward my thoughts although I was somewhat aware of them.

The only one thing I was absolutely sure of was that I was completely helpless. And do you know what the worst part about knowing that you're helpless is? The worst part about knowing that you're helpless is that there is nothing you can do about it. There is a significant difference between feeling helpless and knowing that you're helpless.

When you feel helpless, it's as if you're trapped in a long, dark tunnel with a dim light. No matter how small or dim this light may be, it's there. All you need to do is gather the willpower to find this light to bring a stop to your helplessness. But knowing that you're helpless nearly means that you're trapped in a long dark tunnel devoid of any kind of light, and there is absolutely nothing that you can do to turn on the light. So when you're surrounded by solid darkness, you'll know that you are indeed helpless.

I was helpless. Only an unearthly force had the ability to destroy my despair, but I was sensible enough to not hope for one, as I've never believed in unearthly forces before.

I got Felix out of his cover while Cinder repositioned his head to my knee, as he knew that it was Felix's turn on my lap. I often feel that Cinder wonders why I lack the ability to play the guitar without disturbing his pillow (my legs), but he's a considerate dog and accepts me for the way I am.

I realized that I hadn't blinked for a while and shut my dry eyes for a few seconds. On opening them, I found myself watching a movie of my memories, which was being projected by my mind. The background music in the movie was being provided by Felix and my hand.

Soon after, my mother came out looking for me to take me home. We moved in harmony with her arm across my back without the exchange of words—we each found comfort in each other's silence. She then tucked me inside my bed, though I didn't fall asleep immediately. Instead, I wrote songs under my blanket with the help of the light provided by my phone's torch.

Ten songs down the line, my vision went slightly blurry. I thought that it was time for me to attend to the needs of my eyes by exiting the state of wakefulness. Right when I was about to fall asleep, an excruciating pain spread through my chest faster than fire spreads through an unarmed forest. A hollow scream crawled out of my throat while my thoughts drifted into a different world.

Chapter II

It is a cold summer day, and Will and I are walking aimlessly around Brighton Pier. My right shoulder is secretly giving support to his left.

Will is my older brother. He was diagnosed with stage three pancreatic cancer eight months ago. Since his diagnosis, I've seen his body transform from one that was well built and muscular to one that has gotten skinnier than mine. His face no longer glows in the healthy red manner in which it used to, and his legs constantly hurt him, causing him to limp whenever he tries to walk.

I tuck my arm around his, making it seem like he's keeping me warm. If he gets to know that I am trying to make the task of walking easier for him, he will instantly push me away. Watching his strength deteriorate has made him extremely conscious about his declining ability to do ordinary things.

It has been a while since Will has stepped out of the house, and since it is his twenty-third birthday, I felt like he deserved a normal day away from his numerous machines and doctors. We managed to convince our parents by emotionally blackmailing them, and we're out of the house before they could change their minds.

'*Do you want to get a doughnut or an ice cream?*' I ask Will, looking at his face, which seems to be more relaxed than usual.

He repositions his navy blue earflap beanie (a prerequisite by our mother) to reveal his raised right eyebrow and replies, '*No, I'm good. But I do want you to go on one of these rides.*'

'*Oh, come on! Not the eyebrow!*' I say, getting a little annoyed. Will and I have always had this muscle above our eyes that makes our right eyebrows involuntarily rise up whenever we're desperate for something. We call it '*The Eyebrow Raiser.*'

What's amusing about The Eyebrow Raiser is that it has the capability of lifting our right eyebrows. Will and I are pros at raising our left eyebrows, but when it comes to our right eyebrows, we can't raise them by even a millimetre without The Eyebrow Raiser. So if a right eyebrow is up, it means serious business.

'*I think you're forgetting that it's my birthday. I would've gone on a ride for you had I been in your place,*' he says, while his dimples spread across his face. He knew his way around my head quite well.

I push aside my chestnut-coloured hair, which is continuously being blown onto my eyes by the wind and say, '*I don't understand why you want me to go on one when we've come here to spend some time together. Going up and down on a roller coaster is not going to provide me with any satisfaction if I just sit in it alone.*'

'I'll come with you.'

'No.'

'Why?'

'Are you seriously asking me why, William?' By now, I am starting to lose my patience. I just want a regular day without the cancer that is engulfing my brother's body along with my entire family. I'm scared to even think about it: I don't want Will to have a mid-air heart attack on the rollercoaster.

'It's not like my body will get strained or anything,' he replies in a calm, persuasive tone. 'All we need to do is sit back and enjoy the ride.'

For a while, I just stand still looking at his face while going through all the information my mind has stored—thanks to Google—about physical exertion. Chemotherapy can sometimes weaken the heart, resulting in cardiomyopathy, arrhythmia, and several other heart diseases, but so far Will had none.

'My heart and lungs are perfectly fine according to the reports. You can't disagree with them now, can you?' Will asks, while I try to come up with a reason as to why he shouldn't go on a ride.

The only reason I can come up with is that I am very scared. But looking at his desperate face and thinking about how this could be his last proper outing, I decide to give in. 'Just one ride, Will,' I reply, as a smile slowly spreads across my face, washing away a frown that had developed before.

The last time Will had gotten out of bed was a month ago. It was a miracle that he was standing, let alone walking around. In a book by John Green, I read about 'The Last Good Day': wherein the victim of cancer finds himself with some unexpected hours when it seems like the inexorable decline has suddenly plateaued when the pain is, for a moment, bearable.

I think today is Will's Last Good Day.

As the ride begins, I still feel a little scared for Will, but I realize that it would be better to let go and live in the moment instead of worrying about the future. If it really is his Last Good Day, it's my responsibility to ensure that it's the best Last Good Day he could ever have.

We throw our hands up in the air and shout as loudly as we possibly can, as we go up and down and then up again. There's this moment right when we start to go down the roller coaster for the second time when I look over at Will, and I am so glad that I do.

He has the widest smile I have ever seen on his face, and his eyes have never looked happier than they do in this very moment. The paleness in his face seems to be pushed away by a light pinkness. His arms are rhythmically swaying along the air, while the earflaps from his beanie slap across his face. His cheekbones look like they're about to break since it seems as though his facial muscles are getting overexerted by his gigantic smile. He looks like a small child who's on his first ride ever, understanding what it means to be truly alive.

The pink sky glistens as it moves about us making me feel even fuzzier from the inside. As the roller coaster goes up one more time, Will takes my hand and gently holds it and whispers the way he did when we went for our first ride together as kids, 'You're going to be all right Caity. We're going to be all right.'

When I opened my eyes, it took me about thirty seconds to process my surroundings. I was on a hospital bed in a hospital room with a tube protruding out of my chest. The first thought that came to my mind was that Will was dead.

Chapter III

My eyes were met by an abstract purple and red painting; I had woken up in this room in this very way before. Ten seconds after I was back into my conscious world, Dr Johnathan, who had been my lung doctor ever since I was five years old, entered the room with a wide smile. I forced out a smile as Dr Joe (he preferred being called Joe to Johnathan), sat down on a chair beside my bed.

'Caitlyn, I'm sorry about Will,' he said, checking my thoracoscope and drainage bag. He was trying to avoid my eyes.

I nodded, not knowing how to respond. Will passed away the day before, early in the morning. After having about a hundred people coming up to me to apologize for my loss, I still did not know how to respond. 'How much longer till I can go back home?' I asked Dr Joe.

I often develop Pleural Effusion fluid in the lungs for no particular reason. Dr Joe and his team have tried hard to figure out why this keeps happening to me, but they've never come up with a valid reason.

'One more hour and you'll be done,' Dr Joe replied. 'Your parents just left half an hour ago. They insisted on staying, but I forced them to go back home so that they could get some rest.'

'Thank you,' I said, a wave of gratitude spreading inside me. Dr Joe had always been of great help to me. He was not only a highly accomplished doctor, but also a great friend.

'Don't even mention it,' he replied, hesitating a bit before saying, 'I will, ehm, see you there?'

I responded with a nod. He was talking about Will's funeral that was supposed to take place in the evening. Another two hours of receiving sympathetic looks and squeezes on my shoulders.

I was discharged from the hospital at around four in the evening. Children usually weren't allowed to leave without a guardian, but given my situation, the hospital made an exception.

I was used to my lungs filling up with water. It generally happened once or twice a year. It starts with some heavy pressure in the chest accompanied with pain, and can be prevented by a drug developed by Dr Joe's team if caught in time. Since it didn't cause a major hindrance to my regular life, I never paid much attention to it. Although the place where they inserted the needle to drain the fluid out would often hurt, I didn't face any other problems except for slight weakness.

As I walked past the waiting room, I was painfully reminded of the amount of time I had spent there worrying about Will; I no longer had the privilege to worry about him. While the receptionist at the hospital called for a taxi, I spoke to my mother and told her that there was no way I was going to miss the funeral.

I first directed the taxi driver to my house, so that I could change into 'appropriate clothes' for a situation like this, and also because I wanted to take Cinder along with me. Will would've wanted him to be there as well. Then I made my way straight to the cemetery.

Chapter IV

The day Will died, I woke up in the morning knowing that something was wrong. The day before had been the worst day so far. He had been shaking and was in an incredible amount of pain throughout the day and hadn't eaten a thing. Will had been going through extensive chemoradiation therapy, which had managed to give him Myelodysplastic Syndrome—a bone marrow cancer. This meant he had two cancers. At first, he was fighting to win. Now he was only struggling to survive.

I was too scared to allow my mind to ask itself whether it thought that Will was dead. I just lay extremely still on my bed and stared into the darkness. I guess I was trying to extend the amount of time in my life that I would spend by being uncertain about my brother's death.

There had also been times during Will's sickness when I was too afraid to sleep because I didn't want to wake up to find out that I was brotherless. More importantly, I wanted to be there for Will. I wanted to be there when 'his time had come' or whatever. I wanted to help him go (wherever it is that dead people go if they do go somewhere) in a comfortable way. I didn't want him to feel obliged to suffer any longer for our satisfaction because we all understood that he had been through a lot.

I think the main reason Will survived for as long as he did was not because he was scared for himself, but because he was scared about what would happen to us once he passed away. He was fighting the cancer just for us, even though he knew there was no chance that he could ever win. There were times I could make out just by the strain of his voice how desperately he wanted all of it to end.

He no longer looked the same. His dark brown hair had grown thinner and lighter, the area under his eyes had been converted into shallow craters, which rested on cheekbones that jutted out of his face. Everything about his appearance has changed. Everything except for his eyes, which continued to watch over me in their same old protective manner.

I had woken up with this state of mind a few times before as well during Will's period of sickness. Though this time I knew that something was different, the region under my skin felt different and I felt disconnected with my body. As far as I remembered, I was planning to sleep in Will's room the night before, but strangely, I had woken up in mine. Had my parents shifted me back after finding me asleep beside my dead brother? I didn't know. I didn't want to know.

Have you ever had those unsettling moments where you start to question how everything around you has come into existence, and how you've come into existence? It's not a good feeling. I'd call it 'The Feeling of Insignificance' because that's how it makes me feel—insignificant. It makes me feel like I'm some kind of a toy inside a dollhouse—a meaningless object that lacks importance.

Maybe that is why scientists have spent large amounts of time trying to figure out how this world came into existence. We want to feel that we have a purpose, and that life has a purpose. We want to prove to ourselves that there's a difference between us and the dust particles floating in air, a difference between the living and nonliving. But there isn't. The sense of living and the sense of not living are closely linked to in a way that they can't be differentiated. It's the process of reproduction. The living gives birth to the nonliving. In other words, death is the child and his mother is life.

It was because of these thoughts floating around my head that I knew something was different. Why else would I try to convince myself that there isn't a difference between being alive and being dead?

Chapter V

I felt hollow as I made my way to Will's burial site, as though the little sense of liveliness that I had left had been scooped right out of me. I didn't want to be around people. I wanted to wrap myself around the darkness of my blanket and hear music with Cinder by my side. As I walked toward the coffin, Cinder trotting by my side, I found my parents standing together in a way that painfully reminded me of Will. My dad's shoulder looked like it was supporting my mom's. When they saw me, they pulled me into a deep embrace.

'I'm sorry you had to go to the hospital on top of all of this,' said my mom, while she continued to hold me as her slender body towered over mine.

'It's all right,' I replied because it really was. My lung condition was the least of my worries. 'What time will everyone else come at?'

'They should start walking in in another ten minutes or so,' my dad replied, his voice deeper than it's regular self.

I nodded and looked over at Will's golden-bordered mahogany coffin. I caught a glimpse of his navy blue suit, and was painfully reminded of the last time I had seen him in it when he had been recognized for his extensive research in cell mutation. I tried to avoid the coffin at first, but I then realized that I wouldn't get to see him in person ever again.

I got that he was no longer inside his body. But that didn't change the fact that that was still my brother. He didn't look dead to me; he looked like he was just taking a nap.

I grabbed a chair and sat down next to his body, while my parents went over to talk to my aunt and uncle who were speaking to a priest. They looked exactly the way people from the movies do when they're mourning in their black outfits. This made it harder for me to accept the reality, although it was right under my eyes in the form of my brother's lifeless body.

When my dad had entered my room the day before to tell me that Will had passed away, all he was able to say was, 'It's time.' I didn't know he meant that William was already dead. So I made my way to Will's room, still uncertain about his death, while my dad's footsteps heavily followed mine. When I entered the room, I entered a state of shock. My brother was lying dead in a coffin. I leaned against the wall not knowing what to do. I needed to cry, but my tear ducts refused to work.

My mother came and hugged me, while my dad squeezed my shoulders. They thought that physical contact would ease my pain. It didn't. It just made it worse.

I sat beside Will's coffin for the entire the day with Cinder laying his head on my feet, while people kept coming to give their condolences. I unintentionally failed to acknowledge them because I didn't want to shift my gaze from Will's eyes just in case he opened them. Will's eyes gave me a sense of comfort; they made me feel like I didn't have to worry about anything because they'd always look out for me. They were a blended amalgamation of light and navy blue. The lightness brought out the liveliness of his soul, while the navy blue showed how much he deeply cared about even the littlest of things.

Though he had been dead for over twenty-four hours, I just wanted his vein-covered eyelids to slide up, so that I could feel protected by his eyes. My Eyebrow Raiser tirelessly kept my right eyebrow up.

Chapter VI

The next day, I woke up with the afternoon sun forcing its way through my eyes. As I slipped by the states of unconsciousness, followed by subconsciousness into consciousness, I remembered the commitment I made to an old acquaintance. William's friend, Connor, was finally recovering from a long battle of leukaemia; however, his family's financial instability was still getting defeated by the enemy. I had promised his widowed mother, Mrs Croft, that I would sing in front of her Lebanese restaurant-café, Quhwa, for a couple of hours to attract customers. I knew she wouldn't expect me to keep up with my promise given my condition. But to me, the promise was something that would get me through the dreadful day.

I put on a black sweater, some black pants, and a pair of black boots not realizing the irony till I looked into the mirror. I was black inside out. Trying my best to avoid my parents, in other words, the awkwardness created by our family reducing by a quarter, I reticently slid down the stairs only to find my mother waiting for me in the kitchen.

The sad smile she greeted me with landed on my head, trying to pull me down with its heavy weight. I responded with a hasty glance and poured full cream milk into a white bowl of coco puffs as she closely observed my every move.

'Are you sure you feel well enough to go?' she repeated for the third time since the night before.

'Yes, Mom, I'm sure. I have nothing else to do,' I replied, as my stubborn brown eyes met her light ones.

'You're not wearing enough layers,' she said as she left the room and came back with a knit muffler, which had punches of dodger blue blended into its navy blue skin. It was Will's muffler.

She lifted my hair up, wrapped the muffler around my neck, and tied it into a slipknot just the way I liked it and said, 'This will keep you warm.'

And it did.

I grabbed Felix and my coat, also black, and made my way to Shepherd's Bush. Quhwa was of different shades of brown, which balanced each other just right to produce a strong attractive comforting force. I was told that at one point of time, the cluttering of crockery blended with the pleasant chatter of customers overflowed out of its squared windows. Now suffering the common after-effects of cancer, it was left barren.

As I turned into the restaurant-café's entrance, I was met by Connor's younger brother, Michael. Though he tried to hide it, I could make out that he was stunned to see me there. I'm guessing he thought I was too broken to carry on with life.

'I'm sorry about William. We're all really going to miss him,' he blurted, fiddling with his brown hair, which jotted out of his skull the way a lion's mane does. The only difference between the two was that his hair curved downwards instead of pointing out, and making him look like he's been electrocuted.

I thanked him, trying to kill the awkwardness of the situation I still wasn't used to.

'I'll just set the amplifier up, and then you can get started,' he said, making his way to the small platform they had built for performers.

I followed him and took Felix out of his case, while Michael adjusted the microphone for me. 'Let me know if you need anything. I'll be at the counter,' he replied, forcing out an uncertain smile.

'I will, thank you,' I replied with a genuine smile, assuring him that my brother's death needn't prevent him from smiling.

As I stepped onto the platform, the darkened blue ink sky blanketed itself around me, starting from my arms going all the way down to the soles of my feet. Waves of the thick British accent coming from the adjoining pub were sucked out of my ear as I plucked Felix's *E* string.

Ah, it sounded so good. The *E* string drains the water out of my lungs by pushing in nectar that eases my head. It reminds me that I'm still breathing, existing.

And then I started.

Sometimes, the people who are often the closest to you are the ones who you have a hard time expressing your emotions to. I had never been closer to anyone else in the world than I was to Will. I never had a problem telling him about myself, ranging from my views on narcissistic rap artists to my views on evolution. But I did have a problem with telling him how I felt about him.

All I want is nothing more

I hid my feelings from him because I was trying to hide the reality about his condition from myself: he was going to die soon. Whenever Will and I had those moments in which we both felt overwhelmed, it made me sad. I felt that the reason that we were having so many of those moments in short intervals of time was because we wouldn't get a chance to share them later on during the course of my life because his would've ended. I was afraid of the moments that I loved so deeply.

I died a little bit inside

You don't often find the need to tell someone who you love this much how much you love them because you suppose that they know, but after Will passed away, I realized that when you don't express your feelings, they start to haunt you. He died without knowing how much I love him. When I realized he was dead, I didn't cry. My tear ducts forgot how to operate because my suppressed feelings wouldn't allow them to.

Why'd you leave me?

In the funeral, when everyone around me was crying, all I did was blankly look at Will's face. This caused my red itchy eyes to remain dry for longer than what my head could handle. The thing about crying is that it destroys the heavy cloud of darkness that surreptitiously floats its way into my mind when I'm feeling down. And this cloud, it works in the same way the grey clouds in the sky do.

The cloud soaks in all my worries and emotions; it soaks them in faster than the pages of a dehydrated, aged library book soaked in spilled coffee. Now the problem with this cloud is that just like the library book captures the spilled coffee inside its slim body, the cloud imprisons your sorrows. And once it does this, it remains suspended in your head, coming in the way of your other thoughts and clogging your tear ducts.

The only way to escape from this cloud is to make it rain, so that it transforms into tears that can soothingly slide through your eyes. But I don't know how to figure this way out, so the only option that I'm left with is to wait for this cloud to destroy itself by itself. And as far as I know, I don't think anything in its clear-headed state of mind would like to pull the plug on itself.

Why'd you leave me?

Chapter VII

In the evening when I returned home, the one thing that struck me as I walked through the door was how quiet the house was. I felt like I was walking into vacuum.

As I walked through the doors, I didn't know which part of the house to go to. The living room with its stoned fireplace was welcoming, but it reminded me too much of Will; so did the backyard, the basement, my piano. I didn't want to go anywhere. I longed for the comfort provided by my home, and without Will, I wasn't sure that that comfort still lived.

In the kitchen, I took out a glass from the cabinet and poured myself a glass of water, and then slowly sipped it with my back resting against the kitchen sink while my fingers oddly twitched. I just felt so out of place like a stranger in my own house. Without Will, my house didn't feel like the house I was born into, the house I'd lived in for seventeen years. My eyes fell on the kitchen table, which was surrounded by four chairs. 'We don't need four anymore,' I thought bitterly.

I lingered over that thought for a while, and tried extremely hard to lock the doors of my mind, as I didn't have the energy to deal with it. But since I was so worn out, another thought managed to slip inside anyway. I wanted to leave this place.

When I finally went upstairs to my room, I started getting really frustrated. I stood in one spot and erratically started revolving around it. I did not know what I was doing. I felt like I was in some sort of trance. I wasn't so sure about whether I was thinking straight either. I remembered how my mother once told Will and me about how she had taken off without any warning for a month.

I didn't quite understand her at that point because back then, I was just about the happiest little kid in the whole world, and I couldn't imagine ever feeling the need to take off. But things were no longer the same. I no longer felt the same. It seemed as though at first, my life was a perfectly pieced puzzle, but then someone got jealous of how well my pieces were blended in together. So he/she decided to not only destroy my puzzle, but also to steal some crucial pieces, leaving me with a sense of incompleteness.

'Caity,' my dad's voice interrupted my thoughts. I found him leaning against the door, looking at me with slight amusement mixed with a considerable amount of concern. 'What are you doing on the floor?'

I looked at my crossed legs and realized that I was on the floor, singing with Cinder's head on my lap. 'When did Cinder get here?' I thought. 'I'm sitting on the floor,' I said simply.

My dad's eyebrows collapsed into an inquisitive frown. He wasn't sure of how to respond. This was the first time I had been openly eccentric since Will's diagnosis. My parents already had enough on their hands without my eccentricity.

'It's getting cold,' he said.

'The floor's carpeted with woollen fibres, which have been intertwined so closely that I doubt they'll allow atoms, let alone coldness, pass through them.'

My statement provoked more confused frowning.

'Can I go to sleep now? I'm tired,' I replied, sounding more childish than I thought it was possible for me to.

'Yes honey, you can go to sleep. Are your lungs better? Did you take your Prozac?' he asked.

To make things worse for my parents who had a dying (now dead) son, I was diagnosed with a case of severe depression a few months after William fell sick. Prozac, the antidepressant prescribed by my psychiatrist, was the least effective medicine I had ever taken. But I was forced to continue with it and remain *patient* for the serotonin to kick in.

'I'm good, Dad. The lungs are good. And yes, I did take the Prozac despite the fact that it clearly does not work for me,' I said.

He came over to kiss my forehead, trying to ignore the last remark. 'Let me know if there's anything I can do for you,' he said and left the room, closing the door behind him.

I thought to myself, 'No, there is nothing you can do for me unless it involves getting William back,' and then immediately felt guilty. Why would I say something like that even if it was only in my head?

I needed to get away. I was turning into a monster. What if I let one of my thoughts slip out of my mouth? I could potentially ruin my parents. I hadn't thought about the kind of person I was turning out to be during Will's sickness because who pays attention to themselves when the person who they just about love the most in the world is about to die?

I no longer knew who I was. I didn't know what I wanted from life, and I didn't know who I wanted to be. And not knowing what you want to do, what kind of a person you are, or want to be can drive you insane. It was driving me insane.

I needed to go someplace that was artistically inclined, a place where I could feel like myself again and just connect to myself and to people who were like me even if they'd been dead for years. I felt that Vienna would be ideal for me. It had just about everything that I was looking for: Mozart, Haydn, Music, and Art.

Money wasn't an issue for me because of all the busking that I had done. I've been busking ever since I was around eight years old, and I used to end up making quite a bit of money by playing genres varying from indie folk to grunge to rock. I'd usually donate some of it while keeping the rest of it in a small personal safe at home. By the time I was eighteen, I had saved enough money to pay not only for a train ride to Vienna, but also to survive for about week or so without making more money.

I decided to take Cinder along with me as well. He'd been miserable after Will's death, and I thought that if I took off without him, he'd just feel worse. Also, Cinder was my pillar of support. He'd been with me through thick and thin, and at that time, I needed him more than I ever had before.

I grabbed my favourite backpack and snuck into the storage room to get my small suitcase. I was extremely particular when it came to packing my clothes because I knew that I'd have a problem with wearing unclean clothes—they give me a hard time thinking straight.

I decided to take Felix (obviously) and David (my beautiful solid wood mahogany ukulele), my earphones and iPod, a small, blank sketchbook, two notebooks, two thin-lined permanent black markers for sketching, and my quill, which I used for writing along with a bottle of its ink. I also packed a polaroid photo of Mom, Dad, Will, and me, my copy of 'Every Day' by David Levithan given to me by my closest friend, my laptop, and Cinder's favourite ball along with dog biscuits and a few bones.

The only problem I was left with was that I was worried about my parents being worried. I knew that my parents trusted me completely, and I didn't plan on breaking their trust soon or ever. And I thought that they'd be all right with me leaving for a short while. I knew that my mother definitely would. So I decided to leave a short note for them that said:

> *Dear Mom and Dad,*
>
> *I'm extremely sorry if this gets you worried, but I've decided to go away for just a short while. I haven't been feeling like myself at all lately. This has nothing to do with the two of you so please don't think it does. I have enough money from all the busking so that shouldn't be a problem. And I promise I'll be regular with my meds. I'm taking Cinder along with me. Please don't go around looking for me. I'll be fine.*
>
> *I love you*

And then I left.

Chapter VIII

I anxiously tried to walk as fast as I could toward the bus stop without breaking into a jog. It's a funny feeling, really, when you're all anxious and jittery and you feel too scared to move too fast, but at the same time, you're scared that you're moving too slow and then you end up wobbling more than walking. And the wobbling starts to wobble around the only sanity left in your mind.

When I got to the St Pancras International Train Station, I felt a little more secure. I asked the person at the ticket counter how to get to Vienna, and she looked at me in an odd way. Who wouldn't? I was a 17-year-old girl with a giant dog, spontaneously taking a train to Vienna at 1.30 in the morning. Thankfully, she didn't question me and told me to first get to Paris Nord, and then change trains to get straight to Wien Westbahnof in Vienna.

I made my way to the dark platform twelve where my first train would arrive. I was about ten minutes early, so I decided to sit down on a bench nearby. I took my sim card out of my phone, so that my parents didn't have a way of tracking me down and switched it off.

As I sat down on the bench, I felt the silence and solidarity of the train station taking me into its arms and I let it. In fact, I quite enjoyed it. The metallic earthly air filled me with the sense of thrill as I observed the way the train tracks disappeared into dark tunnels. Above my head, there were twinkling stars, which with each twinkle seemed to fill me with confidence about my decision.

Being at a train station in the middle of the night when no one else is around makes you feel like you've been bestowed upon with power. You can do anything you want with the amount of empty space you have. You could enact a character from your favourite play or you could just think. I mean, you could really think. The kind of thinking one can do in a train station is the kind of thinking that can be done nowhere else. It's not plainly because of the emptiness of the train station. On the contrary, it's about the business that it contains for most of its day. It's about the little time that it gets to itself, which it doesn't even truly get to itself because there will still always be someone inside it just like I was inside it.

A few minutes later, I could hear the train approach, and as its whistle's voice got louder, the excitement building up in my stomach grew stronger. Before I knew it, the train was standing right in front of me waiting for me to hop onto it. As the doors welcoming unfolded in front of me, I took in a deep breath and looked at Cinder and whispered, 'This is it boy, are you ready to hop into our adventure?' He replied with a happy bark, acting as if he understood each word of what I had said.

And then we hopped onto the train.

Chapter IX

When we got onto the next train from Paris Nord Station, I sat on a seat beside a window, and Cinder sat on the seat beside me and laid his head on my lap. I could tell that he was tired, so I stroked his head and softly sang for him till he fell asleep. Aside from the 18-year-old girl and her handsome Labrador, the tube light lit train was deserted. Only two had taken the decision to embark on an Austrian adventure that night.

I was beginning to feel quite unsettled. As I looked outside the window, this wave of nostalgia blended in with sadness hit me, making me feel like as though time was dilating. It wasn't because I was remembering something from the past or because I was going away—I didn't regret my decision for even one moment. Instead, it was due to the speed of the train. The blurry orange lights were passing by fast, making me feel like I was in slow motion. I felt the burden of some missing pieces in the puzzle of my life. Something about William's death didn't seem right. His time had come before it was scheduled to.

I tried to steer my mind away from the commotion it was creating within itself by listening to some music. I took my iPod out and scrolled through my favourite playlist.

My eyes fell upon the song Vienna by Billy Joel, and I immediately decided to listen to it.

Slow Down You Crazy Child my mind whispered to me, while Joel sang the same to my ears. I allowed myself to fall asleep. Vienna had a good ten hours of waiting to do to meet me.

Chapter X

The sun managed to make its way into my eyes half an hour before the train was to reach Vienna. I let out a tiny yawn catching glances of a lonely church, a lethargic gas station, and a football stadium in between squints. I couldn't wait to get off the train and into Vienna. I kept getting flushes of excitement blended with anxiety.

I gently tapped Cinder on his rib cage to wake him up. As he rose from his deep slumber, he planted a soft kiss on my hand. 'Are you ready boy?' I half whispered.

He replied with a sleepy, happy bark.

Cinder always made me feel like he understood each and every word that came out of my mouth. And that wasn't it; he understood how I felt by just sitting next to me. Communicating with him was just about the easiest thing in the world because you didn't even need to spell out your worries to him, he just knew everything.

As we approached the station, the train became slower and my flushes became more intense. The train finally came to stop, and just like that, we were in Vienna.

Chapter XI

When I walked out of the Westbahnhof Train Station, I was hit by the warm welcome of the Mozart-filled Viennese air. I finally started feeling like I was more in control of my life. The incompleteness in my head was reduced by a small amount, thereby taking away the burden of a large amount of anxiety.

I made my way to a cheap hotel that I found online called The Vienna Inn. I only needed to pay fifteen euros for one night. But cheap hotels often come with multiple problems, don't they? In this hotel, I wasn't paying fifteen euros just for a single room; I was paying fifteen euros for a shared dorm with six other people. I was pretty scared about this because I'd never been to a non-luxurious hotel, and I had heard horrifying stories about such hotels in the past.

As I got closer and closer to the hotel, the road no longer felt as though it was a part of the rich country it belonged to. The dark streets echoed with the shrill cry of cat, causing Cinder to frighteningly growl. When I reached the front of the hotel, I decided that there was no way on earth I could stay there. It was in such a bad shape that it looked as though it was about to fall right over my head. In addition, a rusty dimly-lit lamp post loomed over its entrance with the word 'run' hurriedly inscribed on it. And so I did.

I briskly walked toward Kärntner Strasse, one of Vienna's busiest shopping streets, which was about thirty minutes away, to see if I could make some money and then spend the night in a safer place.

I got hold of Cinder's leash in one hand, the handle of my suitcase in the other, and made my way to Kärntner Strasse, not knowing where I was *really* headed.

Chapter XII

Simply put Kärntner Strasse is beautiful. It had everything I was searching for: cafés, opera singers, bassists, it had all kinds of art bursting out of it. The first musician I encountered was dressed as a sailor and was using water-filled wine glasses as his instruments. His fingers bounced and swirled around the rim of the glasses, producing a magical version of Beethoven's fifth symphony. 'This is the place for me to be,' I thought to myself, while giving him a nod of appreciation.

I had heard that one needs a licence to busk in Vienna, and I didn't have one. But I was desperate to start making money. I didn't want to run back home already without achieving what I had come looking for. So I decided to find a spot clear of any police and try busking there for a while. I was a little nervous about doing this because I had always been pretty particular about going by the rules, but I managed to give myself a pep talk. 'This is my once in a lifetime opportunity, and it is in my hands to either grab it or let it miserably slip away,' I said to myself. 'I am at the largest turning point in my life and it demands a change.'

So I gave it a change.

The sky was approaching a deep orange as the atmosphere gently filled up with lightheartedness, a by-product of approaching nighttime. The clock was striding toward five, and the streets were full of tourists. In front of me, a toddler child was delicately swung about by his young parents, who were on either side of him, painfully reminding me of the times I was in his place.

I reminded myself to focus on the present, and found a spot next to a small, pink café that was quite ideal. It was located right under a tree, next to a dark green letterbox. Cinder sat down beside the letterbox, while I opened Felix's hard case and laid it down on the ground so that people could put money in it.

While tuning Felix, I tried to think of what song to start with. It was usually the first song I had a problem choosing because once I started singing, I didn't have to think of what song to play next because the songs seemed to arrange themselves. All I had to do was go with the flow. I finally decided to sing Vienna by Billy Joel. It felt appropriate.

Before getting into the song, I did this default tapping thing that I always did before I played the guitar just to get myself warmed up, and then I started singing. When I started with the verses, there weren't too many people around, but I didn't care because I was completely immersed. My head became lighter, I no longer felt like I was carrying a burden. When I reached the chorus, the burden drifted away entirely; and somewhere in between, I ended up closing my eyes. When I opened them, I was met by about five faces that were actually interested in listening to me sing. One silver-haired couple danced along to my rhythm, filling me up with warmth that pushed me deeper into the music.

More people passed by and put money into Felix's case, while some stood in front of me for a while. But what mattered the most was that I integrated myself with the music, with my conscience dancing along with his rhythm. I smoothly glided from one song to the next, and very soon, the real world was no longer what my eyes were seeing. My eyes were seeing the dancing music and nothing else.

After what seemed to be a short while, I opened my eyes. By now, there were around ten to twelve people standing in front of me and clapping. It was quite overwhelming. I also caught a few clapping hands in the café nearby. I gave a slight bow and thanked everyone.

When I looked at my watch, I was shocked to see that it was already 7 p.m. I suddenly became cautious of the fact that I was supposed to be on a lookout for the police, but didn't spot any. I went over to Felix's hard case to put the money into my backpack. I was so happy I didn't even feel the need to count it.

I got a hold of my belongings and nudged Cinder, so that he would get up and start walking (he could be quite lazy at times). I thought I'd head over to a café to get some dinner, but instead, I was stopped by a tall, dark-hazel-blue-eyed Austrian guy.

Chapter XIII

'Hallo! My name is Theophilus,' said the tall Viennese boy with a thick Austrian accent. His puff of dark brown hair flopped about his black brow line glasses, as he extended his hand forward for a handshake. He was wearing navy blue pants with a navy blue shirt and an orange sweater.

'I'm Caitlyn.' I replied while returning his handshake.

'Caitlyn! I saw you busking, and I must say that I was completely mesmerized by your style,' he said in a loud voice. And then he unexpectedly shouted, 'WOW!'

I let out an embarrassed smile and thanked him. I've never really figured out how to accept compliments.

'Where are you headed?' he asked, while his waist swayed from left to right.

'I was just going to get some dinner.'

'Can I join if that's okay with you?' the swaying got faster now.

'Why not?' I replied with a smile. I was getting tired of talking to just my mind, I needed some human interaction as well.

Theophilus' eyes fell upon Cinder and he led out a tiny yelp. At first, I thought he was scared, but then he sort of jumped down and landed on his heals and started vigorously petting Cinder repeatedly whispering, 'Who's a good boy?'

'That's Cinder,' I said. 'He's going to turn three soon.'

'Awh man, I love dogs!' he replied in a loud voice, and then shouted, 'I love them!'

I let out a small laugh. Theophilus' enthusiasm reminded me of Will in some ways.

He then saw that I had a backpack and suitcase. He pointed at my suitcase and asked, 'Do you plan on running away or something?'

'It's a long story,' I replied. 'I'll tell you over dinner.'

'All right then, we better hurry because I'm a sucker for good stories,' he said with a wide smile.

Theophilus led the way by bobbing up and down on his toes. His heels didn't hardly rested on the cobbled street for more than a millisecond. We decided to eat in the small pink café that was next to my busking spot. I ordered an Americano and Caesar salad, while Theophilus ordered a Marnier and Margarita with mushrooms.

'Okay, I'm dying to hear your story, so please put me out of my misery!' said Theophilus as I sipped my Americano.

'Well, don't get your hopes too high. I'm just like any other regular person,' I replied.

'What I witnessed right now was far from being a regular performance by a regular person. So hush with the modesty, will ya?' he said with a smirk. 'Now go on.'

'Okay, I don't know how to explain this without getting personal and I normally wouldn't,' I began. Theophilus gave me the kind of encouraging look that parents give to their children when they forget their words during a performance. I went on, 'My brother, Will, passed away two days ago. After his funeral, I just couldn't bear to stay in London anymore, that's where I'm from. I needed some time away from everyone else, and so I left.'

I felt guilty after I finished talking because I realized that I had just put Theophilus in an awkward position. All the excitement in his face seemed to have drained away.

'I am terribly sorry,' he whispered. I could make out from his eyes that he really did feel bad.

'Don't apologize, it's not like you killed him,' I said, feeling a little embarrassed.

He let out a slight sigh and looked directly into my eyes. For a second, I got distracted by the way his eyelashes perfectly curled upwards. He then continued, 'Okay, since you just told me something personal about yourself, I should do the same with you. I'm into men.'

'Aw, really? I support the LGBT community,' I replied, glad he steered the conversation into a different direction.

'Oh, thank god you support us. Can you imagine how weird this would have been if you didn't?'

I allowed myself to laugh. He knew how to soothe a tense atmosphere.

'I was almost close to falling for you, but I don't think that's going to be possible now,' I said, smiling truthfully.

'I'm sorry to break your heart. I can't help being irresistible, it's just how I am,' he said with a smirk that highlighted his bony cheekbones.

'Ahh, if only I was a man,' I sighed.

It was then that I realized how long it had been since I had been treated normally. Back in London, I was the girl whose brother had cancer. But with Theophilus, it was different. With him, I was who I really was—an ordinary person.

'So where do you plan to stay?' Theophilus asked, biting into his Margarita.

'I don't know yet,' I replied, realizing that I hadn't thought of a way to avoid spending the night on the bare streets of Vienna.

Theophilus deeply stared at me for a while, while sipping his bitter orange coffee. Then he snapped his fingers, and in an intense voice said, 'You can stay in my place. I live in a one-bedroom apartment, but there's a couch in the living room you can sleep on. It's small but it's clean. You don't need to worry about the rent, I own the place, and you can stay for as long as you want. And that goes for Cinder as well, I've always wanted to live with a dog.'

I was a little thrown off by his offer. Was he really ready to make a life-altering decision for a girl he met on the streets less than an hour ago? I didn't know what to say, and my face probably showed it because he then said, 'Don't worry, take your time to decide. Think about it while you finish with your salad.'

So I ate my salad and he ate his pizza. We didn't say a word to each other for a while. I started thinking about what to do. I had only just met the guy, and I didn't know him at all. He seemed safe, but just because I thought he was friendly, I couldn't trust him. But he understood me so well. He took away the loneliness I had been swimming in for so long. And how long could I possibly bear to live in scary inns with all kinds of murderers, kidnappers, and rapists? Living with Theophilus was the best option I had.

Theophilus was patiently eating his pizza, while looking up at the sky. His downward-pointing slender nose added to the innocence of his face. I finally decided to break the silence by saying, 'Thank you so much for your offer.' He shifted his gaze back to me while I continued, 'But I can't stay with you without paying the rent because that would be unfair. And are you sure you wouldn't have an issue with taking me in?'

'Well, I can't take any rent because if you did pay the rent, it would be rent for a couch and that's absurd. But if you really insist, we can share the water and electricity bill,' he said and continued with a smile spreading across his face. 'And of course, I want you to stay with me. If I didn't, I would've never asked you in the first place. I have great people instincts.'

I looked deeply into his eyes and for a flicker of a second, I spotted a familiar longing behind the haziness of his hazel blue iris—he too was lonely.

'Okay, but you're absolutely sure about having both Cinder *and* me?' I asked, looking for any sign of resentment or hesitation in his face. I couldn't find any.

Theophilus jumped off his chair and leaped beside mine and said, 'I am as sure as I can be.'

Chapter XIV

We turned right from Kärntner Strasse, walked across the bridge that stood on Donaukanal, which is a part of the Danube River. It took us around thirty minutes to get to Arenawiese, the park where he lived.

Theophilus started telling me about how he got down to buying his house. 'Buying apartments naturally requires a lot of money in a place like Vienna even the ones that have just one bed room,' he said. 'At first, I had to pay rent because I didn't have enough money to buy the place. I wasn't planning to either, though I secretly always wanted to. So everyday, I would save some money from street acting. And by the end of five years, I managed to collect enough and my tenant gladly sold it off to me. I'm pretty sure he was happy to get rid of the place.'

Arenawiese was a large, overly grassy park. It was covered with trees that had narrow trunks and small leaves. And right in the middle of the trees was a small, shed-sized house made entirely out of wood, which looked like it was originally meant to be a shed.

As Theophilus opened the door to his home, and turned on the switch to a bulb that was hanging inside near the door, he said, 'It's a small place, but I think you should like it.'

The main door opened into a living room that had a medium-sized couch in the middle with a small table in front of it. The walls and floor were made of wood that made you feel like you were in a tiny cabin. Opposite to the main door were the doors to the bedroom and bathroom. There weren't any lights except for a small lamp on the table and the bulb next to the entrance, but those were just enough. On the right, there was a large window with red curtains that looked all over the grass and on the left there was a small bookshelf that was overflowing with books. It was a *very* small place but I liked it.

'It's beautiful,' I said looking at him.

'I'm glad you think so,' he replied with a proud grin while shutting the door.

It was getting pretty late, so we decided to go to bed. I settled down on the couch with a blanket in the living room, while Theophilus shuffled around in his own room, humming a tune from a song by the band Radiohead.

'Theophilus, what do you do for a living?' I asked after the shuffling died down.

'I write. I write plays, mostly monologues,' he said. I could make out by his voice that he loved what he did. 'I used to act, but I haven't done that in a while.'

'That sounds wonderful. Do you work for someone?'

'I do, I have a job at a theatre in Der Josefstadt.'

'Hey, do you mind if I have some classical music on for the night? I can't really sleep without it,' he said, probably wondering what kind of music I was interested in.

'I love falling asleep to the sound of classical music,' I replied.

I smiled as I heard Moonlight Sonata echoing out of a vinyl player. Vienna already felt like home.

And then I fell asleep in the arms of classical music.

Chapter XV

The next day, I headed out with Cinder to get my busking licence and explore the different ways I could make money. Theophilus went for work and gave me a spare key to his home. I sang on the street for a few hours, and then decided to look for another source of income.

I went to a few bars and cafés to find out if any of them were in search of musicians, but none of them seemed to be interested. After about two hours of jumping from one place to another, I found a bar called Entlang, which was around twenty minutes away by foot from Arenawiese.

As I walked into the bronzed blue wallpaper covered bar, I was met by a middle-aged Austrian man with grey hair on his head and black moustache. He casually drew large puffs from an archaic golden brown pipe. I highly doubted that he'd hire me, but I asked him anyway and surprisingly, he asked me to give an audition. After singing a few songs for him, he told me that he could give me an evening job five days a week with Mondays and Tuesdays off, and offered me a higher salary than I expected.

When I walked out of the bar, I felt relieved. I no longer had to worry about my financial condition, and my life seemed to be falling into place even though it was falling quite oddly.

I bought a few groceries and made some scrambled egg with toast for Cinder. I told Theophilus about my day over some salad, and we headed out for a walk with Cinder.

'I'll introduce you to two of my friends today. I think you should like them. They're twins,' said Theophilus while we made our way to the Danube Canal.

I pulled my coat as tightly as I could around my skinny body. It was getting pretty nippy though I loved the weather.

We reached a secluded stretch of land covered with small trees and stoned walls with blue graffiti away from the more populated regions surrounding the canal. Theophilus introduced me to Cara and Duane who were both mechanical engineers.

'Are you from around here?' said Cara with a light German accent. She was about an inch or two shorter than me with distinct blonde hair and just the right amount of muscles.

'No, I'm actually from London, and I needed a break from it so I came here,' I replied.

'You've come to the right place,' said Duane with a smile that produced dimples. His solid black outfit hung loosely on his skinny frame, but interestingly brought attention to his innocuous face. He was the tallest person I had ever come across.

I liked Cara and Duane. They were really warm toward Cinder and me. The five of us sat down beside a tree and watched the dancing reflection of lights from restaurants on the other side of the canal. Duane told me about his past self and came across as a really open person. Cara, on the other hand, seemed to be more of an introvert.

Duane was in love with the colour black. He appreciated the existence of other colours, but black was his soulmate. He told us that his room had only black interiors. Everything he owned was black, everything.

Duane's parents got divorced when he and Cara were just kids. He talked about how he would hide in his closet because all the screaming and shouting would make him anxious. He'd lie there for hours and started identifying comfort in the darkness that enshrouded him. That's when he realized that black seemed to calm him down and tried to buy only black things.

Cara didn't contribute much to the conversation— probably uncomfortable discussing her personal life with a stranger. I understood Cara. Although I was instantly fond of them, I didn't want to talk about Will or about myself either. I was still trying to figure things out.

As Theophilus and I made our way back home, he told me about how he didn't know where he'd be without Cara and Duane. 'They found me by the river a week after I had come to Vienna,' he explained. 'Till then, I had been sleeping on the streets as I had nowhere to go and barely any money. They not only helped me get a job at Die Josefstadt, but also helped me find this house. I wouldn't be where I am today if it wasn't for them.'

I realized that indirectly, even I wouldn't have been where I was if it wasn't for them.

Chapter XVI

Over the next fifteen days, I got into a kind of routine: after having breakfast with Cinder, I'd head out with him for busking. We usually went to two places to busk every day. Every day, I tried to discover new ones. Vienna's so big that you don't need to worry about finding new places to busk—there's always something or the other happening in each corner.

My favourite spot in the whole city was by a lake in StadtPark. I usually went there alone with Cinder and sat under a large, drooping tree, and read a book or wrote and sang songs or played fetch. The lake produced a green tint by reflecting light from trees whose branches almost touched the damp, crumbly soil. It reminded me of Hill even though the two looked completely different from each other.

After busking for a few hours, I usually took a lunch break followed by a second round of busking. At around 7 p.m., I'd drop Cinder home with his standard dinner: scrambled egg and toast, get ready, and make my way to Entlang. For the first two weeks, I performed in Entlang every day because I had nothing else to do. Martin, the easy-going owner of the bar said that I could club my holidays together if I worked on a non-working day.

Theophilus usually got up around eight to go to the theatre. He'd spend the entire day writing, editing, and rewriting there. His boss, who was the producer of the plays, seemed to love him and would usually give him extra work that was often not even related to writing. But Theophilus loved it anyway. He enjoyed doing anything that was theatre related.

After performing in the bar, I'd head back home to be greeted by Theophilus. We both had dinner together. Our work timings were quite similar. We'd then meet Cara and Duane by the Danube Canal for a few hours. Cara and Duane were not only mechanical engineers but also philosophers. The four of us endlessly talked about everything ranging from the importance of fireflies to what it'd be like to live in a BlackHole while taking turns to stroke Cinder.

We were already into December, and it was getting really cold. We could no longer sit by the river for too long; we instead started spending more time in Theophilus' house around a burning candle on the table in the living room. At times, we wouldn't talk at all. Instead, we basked in our family-like silence. Duane and I often played music together. He with his black accordion, and me with Felix. Theophilus would sometimes join us with his chestnut-coloured violin—that is if he wasn't engrossed in drinking his Mariner—while Cara would lay down beside Cinder and smiled to our notes. As time passed, Cara and I got closer. I learnt that there was a time she was as open as Duane. It was only after a nasty relationship at university that she started keeping herself at a distance, trying to avoid conversations.

After months of isolating myself from all my friends back at London, I was almost back to how I used to be before William's diagnosis.

The one thing my psychiatrist repeatedly told me was how important it was to get into a routine. He even wrote one down for me at one point when I got really bad and spent all my time in bed, which was excessively embarrassing. But now, I had this great routine, full of human interaction and whatnot.

This was good.

Chapter XVII

One morning I was woken up by a high pitched scream, jumping out of Theophilus' mouth. 'I booked train tickets for Salzburg a month ago, I cannot believe I forgot!' he shouted. He was pacing up and down the room as fast as he possibly could. 'I booked two train tickets. I was going to force Duane to come along with me but he bailed,' he continued. 'How on earth could I forget?

'Wait, what if both of us go?' said Theophilus, his voice hitting the roof again. 'Do you think you'll come with me, Caitlyn? It would mean the world to me if you do, it really would. Salzburg is where I'm from, and I haven't visited it in years. I really need to go there.'

It was hard for me to say no to him. His eyebrows were reaching up for his hairline. His eyes watched me as though I had the potential to become their God. I could almost see their hazel colour swirling around their deep blue with excitement. Theophilus had done so much for me, I didn't want to say no to him.

'I'm going to call Martin and ask him for permission, okay? But don't get your hopes up yet,' I responded slowly. I was scared of letting him down in case Martin said no.

'I think he's going to say yes,' said Theophilus with a large smile. Then he spun around his feet and gave me a large hug.

'I said do not get your hopes up!'

He was no longer listening to me. He went to his room and started packing.

Chapter XVIII

Two days later, Theophilus, Cinder, and I arrived at the Westbahnhof train station to catch the train to Salzburg. The high grey ceilings with their dimmed yellow light emitting diode lights reminded me of when I first came to this train station from London.

If you had asked me a month ago whether I'd move in with a pure stranger and then travel with him to visit his hometown, I would've told you that you had the wrong person. I am not a social person. I need time to adjust to people before I make life-altering decisions that involve them. And here I was visiting Salzburg with this guy. God, I had changed.

Theophilus seemed excessively jittery. I wondered if it was because we were meeting his ex-boyfriend, Christopher, at the station. I chose to ignore his nervousness and acted as if everything was normal.

The train was nearly empty, and we had a full compartment just to ourselves. We sat down across each other and Theophilus started telling me a little about his past.

'My parents passed away when I was fourteen,' he said rigidly, as though he was fighting with an ocean of emotions.

My face went blank—my standard reaction to bad things since William was diagnosed with cancer.

'I was made to go and live with my dad's brother and his wife who lived right in the outskirts of Salzburg. But it didn't quite work out with them,' he continued, increasing his pace. 'They didn't really, uh, treat me well. I was never allowed to go out by myself. Not even to the back garden because they were afraid that if I ran away, the police would question them.'

'Coffee?' interrupted an old man with a trolley, peeking his head into our compartment with a wide smile that showcased his golden teeth. He poured two cups of latte macchiato and gave us another golden smile before leaving.

'I always felt a certain kind of tension between my uncle's wife and me. Her presence made me uncomfortable,' Theophilus said, warming his hands with his cup of coffee. 'One evening, my uncle was out for work, and it was just his wife and me at the house. I tried to keep out of her way as much as I possibly could, but when she ordered me to bring her a cup of tea, I was forced to face her.

'So I went inside and laid the tea next to her bed,' he went on. His voice began wavering, while he unsteadily increased the speed at which he spoke. 'Once I was done, I turned around to go outside, and I saw that she had walked over to the door and locked it. I acted as though I didn't notice anything and made my way to the door, but she blocked my way.'

Theophilus brought his latte macchiato up to his lips, but didn't sip it. His hands were shaking too hard. I stretched my hand out toward his to stop it from shaking and almost told him to stop, but he went on, staring intensely at the window as though he was watching it happen all over again.

'She walked toward me, started touching me all over. Her hands were soon all over my, uh, area and I was so frightened that I just stood still and waited for it to get over.'

Theophilus pulled down his brow line glasses from his head to his nose, avoiding my eyes. 'When she finally left me, I went to my room and laid down on the bed. I didn't get any sleep because I was frightened that she'd come for me again. I waited till my uncle returned and till they went to bed. Then I grabbed whatever little I had left and ran to Vienna.'

Theophilus stared down at his coffee, which was no longer steaming hot. I watched him for a while, and then got up from my seat and sat next to him, our arms nearly touching.

'I'm so sorry,' I whispered and stared down at his coffee along with him.

Chapter XIX

We went through the rest of the journey without exchanging more words. There was nothing more left to be said for now.

When we reached Salzburg, we were met by Theophilus' ex-boyfriend, Christopher. Christopher was tall and well built with dark hair and a distinct Persian nose. He walked over to Theophilus and gave him a tight, warm hug.

'Theo, I have missed you so, so much,' he said looking overwhelmed. 'Man, you've become even skinnier. Have you been eating at all?'

Christopher looked at Theophilus with concern. He seemed to really care about him.

'Of course I've been eating, don't you worry about me. Tell me, how have you been?' asked Theophilus patting his shoulder, readjusting his attitude to the way it was before he told me about his molestation.

'I've been doing great,' he replied and then looked over at me. 'And who's this lovely lady?'

'This is Caitlyn, she's from London. She lives with me,' said Theophilus, forcing a wide smile.

Christopher extended his hand. 'Hello Caitlyn, I'm Christopher. This one's a hyperactive little child, isn't he?' he said to me while looking over at Theophilus.

'He's all right,' I responded with a grin.

'Okay, so I don't know about you two, but I am starving. How about we grab some lunch from a café close to Salzach?' said Christopher.

Theophilus looked at me waiting for a response. 'Yes, let's go! I'm pretty hungry as well,' I said.

Christopher directed us to his black sedan and drove to Dreifaltigkeitsgasse, a street next to the Salzach River. We found an Italian café and decided to eat there. We took our seats and ordered some food. Theophilus asked for some of his traditional orange coffee liquor to which Christopher said, 'So you've started drinking Marnier like your old man, have you?'

Theophilus smiled, but said nothing.

Chris started looking concerned again and I could make out that he was steering toward an intense conversation. 'Theo, what happened? I still don't know where you've been, and what's been happening with you. I've been worried.'

'Nothing happened, Chris,' said Theophilus. He started fidgeting with his glasses. He couldn't decide whether he wanted them on his nose or his head. He kept touching his head in a way that was worrying. It was obvious that he had no intentions of participating in this conversation.

'It wasn't just *nothing*,' Chris's voice started rising. 'You disappeared for five years. All I got was one mail. That's it. One mail with the four words, "I'm now in Vienna". You think I don't deserve more than four words from you?'

Theophilus didn't respond. All he did was stare at the table, taking small, steady sips of his Mariner. How could he not tell Christopher about what happened at his uncle's house when he told me—a complete stranger in comparison?

'Do you know that I went to Vienna to search for you? That too, three times?' said Christopher with a hint of past despair in his voice. This caught Theophilus' attention.

'One time I almost spent a month, but there was no trace of you anywhere,' continued Christopher bitterly.

'I did not know that,' replied Theophilus quietly.

'You could have stayed with my parents and me. My parents were going to ask your uncle if you could stay with us, but you'd already left with them,' said Christopher, still trying to search for answers.

Our waitress came with the food, but no one seemed to be hungry anymore. She briskly set everything down at the middle of the table and left, sensing the tension suspended around us.

Theophilus remained quiet and started chewing on his pizza while Chris waited. I awkwardly stared at Cinder who was sitting at my feet. After realizing that he needed to respond to Chris, Theophilus tiredly said, 'It's in the past now. I don't want to dig it all back up now. Things happened at my uncle's place. I wanted to come back for you, but coming back to Salzburg wasn't an option because I didn't want them to find me. I really am sorry.'

'What things, Theophilus? Why can't you just tell me what happened?' said Christopher who looked like he couldn't comprehend anything.

'Theophilus, I think you can tell him. He deserves to know,' I said as gently as I can, realizing that that was the first time I opened my mouth since I ordered my mushroom risotto.

For the first time since I met him, I saw anger in Theophilus' eyes. I made a mistake, I pushed him too far.

'You have no right,' Theophilus growled, his ears turning crimson red.

'I'm just trying to—'

'What? Help?' he cut me off. 'You think that you really know anything about me, and what I've been through? I should've never let you in my house in the first place.'

'Theo, calm down, you're overreacting,' Chris said cautiously. He too was surprised by Theophilus' reaction.

'She's overstepping!' Theophilus yelled. I can now see his cheeks are heating up and his hands are shaking.

'Fuck you both!' he said in a strained whisper and stormed out.

Christopher watched him go before turning back to me.

'I'm sorry, I did overstep. I shouldn't have opened my mouth,' I said, heat rapidly rising in my cheeks.

'No, it's not your fault. Why don't you finish up with your lunch, and I'll drop you off by the river. I'm pretty sure he'll be there,' Christopher replied. His voice shrinking into a small size.

I nodded and ate in silence. I was so mad at myself. It wasn't like me to push myself into somebody else's business. But Theophilus did make me a part of this by telling me all about it. How was I supposed to ignore them and act as though I didn't know anything? I felt bad for Christopher. He came across as such a lovely person. And I could see that he really did love and care about Theophilus. And I did too.

Chapter XX

After we finished lunch, Christopher refused to split the bill and paid for it all by himself. As we walked toward the Salzach River, which was just a few minutes away, he handed me a bunch of keys and said, 'I've been looking after Theophilus' parents house, which is now his. The authorities gave me a spare key, so that I could keep it maintained. They have other stuff with them as well, which he can collect. Will you please let him know?'

I nodded as we reached a bridge that was covered with locks, most of which were branded with two names inside sloppy hearts made by permanent markers. There were couples of all ages everywhere, giggling into each other as they made their contribution to this great bridge of love.

Christopher pointed to a skinny figure under the bridge. 'There he is,' he said heavily. Theophilus was sitting with his arms around his legs and his face buried deep into his knees with a lit cigarette in his hand. I had never seen him smoke before.

'Are you sure you don't want to come along with me?' I asked, feeling bad for both of them. It wasn't fair for

Christopher to wait so long to meet Theophilus, only realize that the Theophilus he knew back then isn't there anymore.

'No, you go. I'll just make it worse,' his voice strained as he walked away without looking at me.

As Cinder and I headed toward Theophilus, I saw a red poster that gave instructions on how to connect to your inner self, while sitting by the water. It's golden italic font read 'Close your eyes. Forget yourself. Lose all sense of time.'

The river was embanked by weeds with small, white flowers and large rocks on either side. I walked steadily toward Theophilus like an animal trying to capture her prey. Any quick movements, and he might run away, leaving me stranded under a bridge of lovers.

It wasn't till I was five feet away that he looked up as Cinder galloped toward him full of love and excitement. After receiving the most generous lick a dog can give, Theophilus was forced to let out a decent smile.

'I smoke when I get worked up,' he said, offering me a Marlboro Light cigarette, which I refused. My lungs didn't need any additional damage.

'I was out of line and completely unethical,' I blurted, as he shifted his gaze toward me. His eyes looked tired and small as though he hadn't slept for days.

He let out a sigh and gestured for me to sit down beside Cinder who was now on his back enjoying every single blade of grass. It really was a beautiful place. Beams of sunlight gracefully danced along the river in front of us, while white seagulls glided along the surface. The grass with its pure form of green added to the prettiness of the river with my euphoric retriever.

After a while, Theophilus broke the silence by saying, 'I think we should close our eyes, forget ourselves, and lose all sense of time.'

He laid down on his back and flattened his legs out, and I did the same with Cinder's leash in my hand.

And then we lost all sense of time.

Chapter XXI

B y the time we walked back to Theophilus' house, the sun had been replaced by a crescent moon and a few twinkling stars. Bright yellow lights shone through house windows, warming the aggrandizing cold of December, and revealing children crowded around Christmas trees with handfuls of decorations.

Theophilus' house was made of wood just like his home in Vienna. The driveway went on to the main entrance, and was surrounded by grass on both sides. On the right side, there were two swings, and on the left were young trees and flowers.

As we walked into the driveway, Theophilus' expression changed entirely. Since we reached Salzburg, he'd just been quiet, but now he looked afraid in a depressed way.

He slowly walked to the main entrance and stopped when he reached the porch and took a deep breath. Before I could give him Christopher's spare key, he opened the door with a key that he took out from his pocket. He still kept it with him after all these years.

The inside of Theophilus' house was again, in some ways, similar to his home in Vienna. On the left ran a long window cut short by a door that opened into the middle of the lawn. On the immediate right was a wooden staircase.

The living room had warm sofas with large cushions, all facing rustic fireplace. As I walked into it, I entered a trance on seeing the large oil painting made on a rich navy blue wall. It had one large hand filled in with blended shades of comparatively lighter blue, protruding from one side, which was met by a hundred other smaller hands of the same shade.

Do you know how when you listen to one of those songs you can really connect to, you sometimes feel like you're flowing along with the song? As if every breath you take depends on the next note, as if the next note has the power to pull you up or lay you down? Well, that's how I felt when I saw the hands—overwhelmed.

'My mom made that,' Theophilus said, walking toward the painting and then pointing toward the big hand. 'She said this represented my hand, which reaches out to others through my plays.'

I remained quiet. Nothing I say could ever do justice to this piece of art.

We then made sandwiches from a variety of cheeses and vegetables in the fridge, which had probably been stocked up by Christopher.

We ate our dinner in silence. It had been an emotionally exhausting day for Theophilus. Though there were three bedrooms upstairs, we ended up sleeping on the couches because Theophilus wasn't comfortable going up to his parents' room.

I couldn't help but think about what it would be like for me to return home.

Chapter XXII

The next morning, we decided to head back to the Salzach River to see it one last time as we were returning to Vienna in the evening. Theophilus still hadn't gone upstairs to his bedroom and his parents' bedroom. But before we left, he decided to quickly run up to get something from his room, while I waited on for him in the driveway.

I walked around the left side of the garden that had been partitioned from the right by a cemented path. The trees and flowers looked like they had been watered regularly. I then went and sat on one of the swings and swayed back and forth. On the wooden pole, supporting the swings, I saw a small engraving that said, 'Chrisophilus.'

Theophilus came back down with the most beautiful golden music box with his name carved out on it. 'It plays Moonlight Sonata,' he said. 'My grandma gave it to me when I was just a little boy. It used to help me fall asleep every day.'

He saw me noticing the engraving and said, 'Christopher and I built this swing set from scratch. He wanted to name it Christopher Junior, which I thought was absurd, and I wanted to name it Theophilus The Second. After many heated arguments, we decided to merge our names and settled on Chrisophilus.'

He looked at the entire swing set from it's bottom where it had been implanted into the ground to its top where a solid plank supported to metal swings. 'Let's get out of here,' he sighed, trying to hide any hint of pain in his voice.

The three of us made our way down the embankment and sat on a rock under the bridge right where we sat the day before. Theophilus had his Mariner, Cinder had his favourite ball, and I had my Americano.

A gentle, cold breeze that ran along with the flow of the river softly grazed my cheeks. I felt the most relaxed I had in years. All the strain that had been tightening inside my head since Will got cancer began to unwind. I would lie down beside that river for the rest of my life if I could.

'Now that we're at it, I might as well tell you about my parents,' Theophilus said, taking in a deep breath.

'Fire away, I can take it,' I say through a sympathetic smile.

We were getting back to the way we were before the train ride to Salzburg. In fact, I felt as though he was becoming more comfortable with me because he started opening up a lot more. This made me feel guilty since in comparison to the things I knew about him, he hardly knew anything about me at all.

'They passed away in an accident,' he said grimly. 'They had gone out to meet some friends of theirs while I was at home.' He sipped at his Mariner and said, 'My dad was a lawyer. A well renowned law firm had just hired him, and he was beginning to do really well. My mom, on the other hand, was an artist.' He continued with a slight smile, 'She loved making things disproportionately like the hand you saw in the living room wall. I love disproportionate art.'

He then shifted his gaze toward Cinder and started stroking his head. He no longer wanted to meet my eyes. 'The day they passed away, I was trying to prepare a monologue about a boy with multiple personality disorder for the Salzburg Whitsun Festival. I was just getting started when the phone started ringing. I hopped over to the other end of the house toward the phone, a million thoughts about the play running through my head.'

Theophilus set his Mariner on the grass, and anxiously started fidgeting with his glasses again. The story was beginning to get tougher to narrate.

'I answered the call, and at first, all I could hear was disturbance,' he continued. 'I was almost about to cut the call when I heard the voice of a lady. She said urgently, "Am I speaking to Theophilus?"

'"Yes this is Theophilus," I said while my thoughts came started slowing down to a stop. I could feel that something was different. "I'm so sorry, your parents have been in an accident. I'm a nurse speaking from Salz Hospital," she said. The air around me seemed to come to a stop as my body went rigid. I went blank. I somehow grabbed my coat and then ran for the hospital. A receptionist took me to a trauma room with my father in it. He was covered in blood. It was all coming from his head. How can someone's head have so much blood that it drenches his entire shirt?' he said, his voice was beginning to strain, his face slightly scrunched. 'A nurse came out of the room and told me that they were going to take him for surgery. They didn't even let me say goodbye to him.'

Theophilus held his head with his right hand, his left hand still stroking Cinder while his eyes fought back tears. 'My mom was already in surgery due to lung failure,' he continued. 'I was directed to a waiting room and told that I'd be informed about my parents' conditions shortly. The wait was never ending. I felt sick throughout,' he said, burying his face into his knees. 'After about two hours, some neurosurgeon came to talk to me. He told me that my dad was in a coma because the damage was far too profound, and they weren't able to control the swelling. He said that there was a high chance that Dad wouldn't ever wake up and left me to digest the news. Then my mother's doctor followed by my dad's neurosurgeon came to give me an update,' he went on with his head now resting on his knees, and his face hidden with his arms. 'My mother's lungs were no longer viable to keep her alive, she needed donor lungs. And they wanted me, a 17-year-old, to decide whether I wanted to terminate my dad's life to give my mom's a shot. They hadn't even declared him brain dead, they left it up to me to decide.

'I tried to sit but I wasn't able to. I tried to stand, but I wasn't able to do that either. I was on the verge of losing everything. I know my dad would've wanted me to make sure that his lungs reach my mom. And my mom would've wanted me to wait for my dad to wake up. I was forced to favour my dad's wishes because the doctors were almost sure that he wasn't going to wake up. I wanted to wait so badly, I couldn't bear to make the decision of pulling the plug on him, but I did. And I wish I could go back and change my decision because my mom's body refused to accept the lungs. She was on the ventilator for three days after which her body gave in.

'I lost both my parents in a matter of a few days, and I'm sure I could've saved at least one of them.'

We both sat in silence for a minute or two with our arms wrapped around our knees, watching white seagulls playing along with waves of water. I wanted to tell him he made the right call, but I knew he wouldn't want to hear that, so I focused on my Americano and the seagulls.

'It really is beautiful, isn't it?' he said with a sigh, as playful waves gushed past. He then got up and walked further down toward a rock that's lower half was submerged into the water. He signalled me to follow him and I did.

As I got closer to the rock, I saw that someone had scribbled on it with a black marker. It said, 'I don't think we have much to complain about if we're meant to swim against the current because that would be one gorgeous swim.'

'One day when I came here with my mom because I was having a hard time with the whole gay thing,' said Theophilus, as he ran his fingers along the words, which looked like they were always meant to be on the rock. 'All we did was stare at the river, and that alone made me feel better. And then she turned to me and said, "You know what, Theo?" But she didn't complete her sentence. Instead, went over to the rock and scribbled onto it with her black marker. She always had a black marker with her, she was obsessed with them. Then she made me read it and believe it.'

I have to say, I kind of believed her as well.

I reached out for Theophilus' left hand from my right and didn't let go till it was time for us to catch our train back.

Chapter XXIII

On the train ride back, I told Theophilus a bit about my brother. Will was an incredibly smart guy. He was studying to be an oncologist and had begun research before becoming a doctor. He had always been ahead of his class even though he barely ever studied what was taught in school. Instead, he spent most of his time learning about how everything else worked.

When he found something of interest, he'd go on for days without sleep, burying himself under books. He would only come outside his room to make coffee for himself and would pat me on the head if he happened to come across me. I think he mistook me for Cinder.

When he did this for the first time, my parents actually got worried and took him to a psychologist after which they realized that their son wasn't a guy with a mental illness. He was just a guy with an extremely high order of thinking.

As we approached Vienna, I could feel my lungs get heavier, though I managed to convince myself that that was just because I missed Will.

'Are you all right?' asked Theophilus, realizing that something was wrong.

I nodded and assured him that I was fine. But as we walked back home, I could feel the pressure building up in my oesophagus; and by the time we reached home, I could barely speak. On entering the house, I reached out for my medicine, which I had kept in my backpack, and in a strained voice told Theophilus about my lung problem.

'Are you sure you don't need to see a doctor?' he said getting worried.

I told him that I didn't because the medicine often worked; and also because I hated going to doctors and hospitals.

I took my medicine and settled down into the couch, and again told him that he had nothing to worry about after which I reluctantly drifted off into a different world.

Chapter XXIV

I'm six years old again and I'm walking around the house looking for something to do. As I walk past my parents' room, I overhear them talking.

'I was watching My Sister's Keeper, and I didn't realize that Will was standing by the stairs and watching it along with me. I don't know how much he saw but I'm worried about him now. He's so sensitive,' says my mother to my father.

I don't wait to hear what my father has to say. Instead, I run outside to the cold, sunny garden to find Will. I want to know what this Sister's Keepers is. I find him on a red swing, but he isn't swinging, he's just sitting.

'Hi Williii-am,' I say in a swing along voice. I just learnt that his full name is William. I like saying William.

'Hi Cait-lyyn,' he replies, mimicking my voice, causing me to giggle. William always makes me laugh. He's the funniest person I know.

'What is this Sister's Keepers?' I ask, trying to remember what the exact name was, while fiddling with his dodger blue muffler.

'*Where did you hear about that?*' Will questions, looking confused.

'*Mommy and Daddy were talking about it.*'

'*Oh.*'

'*Tell me what it is William. I want to know.*'

'*I'm sorry Caity, you won't understand,*' Will says apologetically.

'*I will, Will, I'm smart. Please tell me, it can be our secret,*' I reply, giving him a hug so that he tells me.

'*All right Caity. I haven't told anybody else this, you're the first okay?*' William says, placing me on his lap and turning me toward his light navy blue eyes. '*You won't understand what it means right now, but I'll still tell you. I want to be an oncologist.*'

'*An ocolgist? What is an ocolgist?*' I say, tilting my head.

'*An oncologist is like a powerpuff girl fighting against a mojojojo trapped in someone else's body.*'

I laugh out loud and squeal through my laughter saying, '*Wiiilliiam*' and gently push his large face with my hands. '*You're going to be a powerpuff girl? Which one?*'

'I'm not going to be a powerpuff girl, I'm just going to do something similar to what powerpuff girls do,' William explains looking at me.

'But, but what if you get hurt, Will? The powerpuff girls get hurt a lot,' I say beginning to get worried.

'I won't get hurt Caity, I promise,' William replies, holding me close, gently swinging back and forth.

No, that's not true, I thought while drifting back to the state of wakefulness.

Chapter XXV

As I opened my eyes, I saw that Theophilus was awake, sitting on a chair beside me—he almost scared me. A wave of relief seemed to spread across his face when he saw that I had opened my eyes.

'You scared the hell out of me,' he replied, looking concerned.

'How long have you been sitting here for? What time is it?' I croaked.

He looked at his watch and then looked at me, 'It doesn't matter. Are you okay?'

'I'm fine. This happens to me quite often in the winters. Please get some sleep now, I really am all right.' I felt guilty for keeping him up for so long, but he refused to leave my side. He prepared some hot chocolate for the two of us, and for a while, we sat in silence, taking slow, small sips.

The dream that I had just had made me feel exhausted. I don't like dreaming—it always tires me. This time, it particularly affected me because the dream felt so real. I almost always know the difference between reality and a dream, but when I dream about William, I don't. When I dream about William, I feel like he's right there with me. I can somehow feel his non-existent presence. And getting back to reality and away from Will means getting back to a world full of desperation. After waking up, I just cannot push away the despair of wanting to be with my brother again.

'When you're dreaming, do you feel like you're never entirely happy?' I asked Theophilus, breaking the silence.

'What do you mean?'

'When I dream of something that would make me happy, I don't quite feel completely happy. Instead, I feel a kind of happiness that is blended in with sadness. It's always an incomplete feeling. It makes me afraid of falling asleep.'

'Hold on for a minute,' said Theophilus as he got up to get something. He returned with the golden music box that he got from his room in Salzburg. As he turned the knob, he said, 'I've always been scared of falling asleep to nightmares. But ever since my grandma got this for me, I've had less trouble sleeping because it's almost always managed to keep the bad dreams away. Try to sleep if you can, I'm right here. And if you sleep, I promise that I'll sleep as well.'

I smiled. William always heard Moonlight Sonata when his high order of thinking drove him insane.

Theophilus set the music box, which was now softly playing Moonlight Sonata, beside me. I smiled and rested my head on my pillow, while Theophilus laid down on the carpet where he had made a temporary bed.

Chapter XXVI

The next morning, I woke up to the sound of heavy rainfall. I looked out of the window only to see a blur of water sliding down the glass. The water droplets were coming down with the kind of speed that would enable them to almost penetrate through your skin despite surface tension.

Theophilus was still asleep on the carpet with Cinder lying beside him. I reached out to David, my ukulele, and set him on my lap. I loved playing him on rainy days. He had the power to create a perfect balance between the dreariness of rain and the happiness in his strings.

My head started to feel a familiar pain. The music box, which was still playing Moonlight Sonata, started sounding louder and louder to my ears. I tried to concentrate on David, but I wasn't able to. The pain got more intense, bringing a pressure along with it. I could feel it pressing against my temples. It was beginning to drive me crazy.

I got up to search for some Aspirin, but couldn't find any. I was beginning to get really frustrated. I was about to wake Theophilus up to ask him for some Aspirin before my eyes fell onto the music box, bringing back a series of images in my mind.

I ran out of the house oblivious of the rain hammering against my head.

Chapter XXVII

I ran as fast as I possibly could, past the never ending rows of trees of Arenaweise and onto the bridge across Donaukanal. I almost stopped to comfort my cold, aching lungs, but then realized that I couldn't stop. Because stopping meant paying attention to my thoughts, and I was not ready for that. So I continued to run.

I no longer knew where I was going till I nearly collapsed in front of a lake surrounded by trees with dropping branches. I realized that this was the lake in Stadtpark—my favourite spot in all of Vienna.

I was too weak and cold to keep my thoughts from engulfing my mind. I had to let them in, I no longer had a choice.

Chapter XXVIII

During his research at university, William came across a drug called Agrenalin, which his professor had been working on. It was similar to morphine. It was an intensive painkiller that made death faster and easier. It had to illegally be made at home.

To make it, I had to buy a variety of medicines—most of which had conveniently been prescribed to Will for his pain. It took about a week to prepare. I had produced multiple batches and followed the instructions to making it as precisely as I possibly could. The first few batches weren't too good, but after I'd produced a few batches, I was certain that I had reached my best and couldn't do any better. I carefully disposed all the batches except for the best one.

It was late in the night, probably 3 a.m. or something, I remember going up to Will's room with a tourniquet and a syringe of my self-made Agrenalin in my hand. I stood at his door and watched him sleep for a while. His breathing pattern was so irregular that it made me tense. I was scared that he would stop breathing at any moment. Even at that moment before I was pushing him toward death, I wanted him to stay forever.

As I walked toward his bed, my chest started to get heavier, and I could feel it getting congested. I sat on the chair beside his head and watched his face, which glowed due to his night lamp.

His cheekbones looked like they were going to pierce through his skin. His eyes looked like they never wanted to open again and had large dark circles under them. I held his hand in mine, although it was extremely frail, it still had the power to spread warmth down my chilled spine. I forgot about how lightly Will had started sleeping and almost jumped when he opened his eyes. He saw the syringe in my hand, but didn't say anything.

'I followed the instructions as well as I could,' I said in a mechanical voice, trying to fight every emotion that was eating me alive. William had been after me for two weeks to end his life till I finally agreed. I was the only one who could put him out of his misery as gently as possible.

He extended the wrist with a cannula toward me. He constantly had drips sending fluids down his body. I was close to crying, but my tears remained in my eyes.

'I don't think I can do this, Will,' I said with my voice shaking all over the place.

'You can. I know I'm being selfish, but if you don't do this with an injection, I'll end up taking my life in a horribly morbid way. And I don't want Mom and Dad to know,' he said painfully.

I nodded, trying to avoid his eyes.

He reached out of my hand and pulled me into a hug. I couldn't fight the emotions anymore, it was all too much. 'You're not selfish,' I sobbed into his shoulder.

I thought my real brother, the one who enjoyed living, and the one who wasn't as frail as a 90-year-old man was gone long ago. William was under torture, his body was being burdened by a tremendous amount of strain every second of his life. His body had given up on him.

I wrapped the tourniquet—a band that makes the veins pop out—around William's arm. Then I straightened myself out and got hold of the syringe. My hand started trembling, but Will held it steady.

'Hold on,' I said, pulling my hand away from his and taking my phone out. I searched for Moonlight Sonata in my music library and put it on at a low volume.

William smiled, his eyes filling up with tears. I knew the music would give him the much needed relaxation.

I put my left hand into Will's right one and held onto it after giving it a tight squeeze. I looked into his light navy blue eyes for one last time. He nodded reassuringly and told me he would be fine and told me he loved me. I told him I loved him too. I steadied my grip on the syringe

And then, I killed my brother.

Chapter XXIX

My eyes were heavy, and I didn't want to open them, but I felt like I needed to just to confirm that I wasn't blind. As my eyelids parted a few millimetres, I realized my terrible mistake. It was too bright. But then I heard a voice. It sounded like a woman's voice, but I wasn't sure. Where was I?

'It's all right, I've shut the blinds. You can open your eyes now,' said the voice.

'No,' I croaked. My voice didn't sound like my voice at all. When did it get so hoarse?

'Trust me, you can do this,' the voice repeated. By now, I was sure it was a woman's voice. It was far too high to be a man's voice.

I gave it another shot. And she was right, it wasn't as bright as it was before. I blinked several times before I could start discerning my surroundings. At first, I only saw purple and red. But I soon realized the purple and red were from an abstract painting in front of me. I looked down and saw a translucent cream coloured tube protruding out of my chest. I turned to the right and saw a nurse standing in front of me, smiling politely, the way most nurses do. I looked around and there was nobody else.

'Am I in London?' I asked, already knowing the answer to the question. This was the hospital room I always found myself in after passing out from a lung episode.

The nurse nodded and said, 'Yes, you are. You've been out on medicines for a day. What is the last thing you can remember?'

That was not a good question. I started freaking out. I tried to move various parts of my body, but I couldn't—everything hurt.

'Where's Theophilus?' I yelled, though my voice was small.

'Your friend is waiting outside. Should I get him in?' she asked.

I nodded, my eyes filling up with tears.

Theophilus came in, trying to look positive but failed. He sat down beside me and touched my hand. His eyes were reddish, he needed sleep.

'I killed Will,' I said, tears streaming down my eyes. This was the first time I had cried since the night I took Will's life.

'What?' he said, looking confused.

I told him everything from the time Will asked me to euthanize him to the time I did and how after killing him, my brain temporarily erased my memories of preparing the Agrenalin and taking his life. The Moonlight Sonata that played out of his music box was probably what triggered back the forgotten memories.

Running away to Vienna now made sense. I was searching for the missing piece of the puzzle, and I had finally found it.

'Are my parents here?' I asked before he could say anything to justify the horrid thing I had done.

'They're waiting outside,' he responded. 'They're worried, but they want you to take your time before you meet them since you ran away.'

'I'll have to tell them, won't I?'

'That's for you to decide, Caitlyn. You can't possibly think that you actually—'

'Don't,' I cut him off, my voice rising. 'I murdered my brother, and I don't need you to tell me I did otherwise.'

Dr Joe entered, grinning, which seemed ridiculous, but I tried to cool down for him. He told me how my lungs couldn't reach out for oxygen, sending me into Hypoxemic Respiratory Failure. Fortunately, Theophilus had been running after me as soon as I slammed his door shut, waking him up. So he called the ambulance and my parents, who flew to Vienna and got me back to London in a helicopter. With oxygen therapy, which reached me in time, there was no permanent damage done.

'Your parents are waiting to see you,' Dr Joe said gently. 'Can I bring them inside?'

'Can I get a few more minutes with Theophilus?' I asked.

'Sure,' he replied, smiling at Theophilus.

'Thank you for coming after me,' I said to Theophilus after Dr Joe left the room. 'My parents couldn't possibly deal with losing one more child.'

Theophilus pursed his lips and stared at me for a while, probably contemplating whether he should touch the topic about my brother's death again. To my relief, he let it slide by.

'I think I need to face the reality of my situation,' he said with a sigh. 'It was hard watching you nearly die. And it's made me realize that I need to sort out things with Christopher. There's never enough time, and I've already wasted a lot of mine. I'm catching a train to Salzburg this evening.'

He pursed his lips again and softly smiled. 'This may sound weird, but thank you for coming into my life Caitlyn,' he said, continuing to smile as he spoke. 'I've been living inside my own world for too long and spending time with you has made me realize that I need to fix the things that sent me down this abyss in the first place. I've decided to go back to school. I'll apply to universities in America to get back to acting and continue with my writing. And I'll try out for Broadway,' he continued. 'After my parents passed away, I forgot about my admission into Julliard and everything else. But watching you play music has reminded me about how my dream of acting on stage hasn't faded away yet.'

'I'm happy for you,' I said with a genuine smile.

We sat there for another minute till my smile started fading. 'I think I should talk to my parents now,' I said, trying to fight off the tears. Once my tap starts flowing, it's hard to get in under control.

'I'll go call them. I spoke to them for a while. They seemed wonderful,' Theophilus said. 'I'll be waiting outside if you need me. My train leaves in two hours, but I can go tomorrow instead of tonight if you want.'

'No, we can't let Christopher wait any longer. You need to go and get your happy ending in order for me to hope for mine,' I lied. There was no happy ending for me. I didn't deserve one.

'Is this goodbye then?' Theophilus sighed.

'For now, yes,' I said sadly, still fighting off tears. 'Thank you for giving me a home when I needed one the most.'

He gave me an awkward hug, trying not to kill me by pressing against the tube.

'Are you going to be fine?' I asked, as he pulled away and walked toward the door.

'Are you?' he said with a raised eyebrow.

'I guess we'll have to wait and find out, won't we?' I said, not sure how I felt about that.

Ten seconds later, my parents were at my side and all three of us were a giant sobbing mess. I looked into their frail eyes and wondered if they were strong enough to face the truth.